Bookings, sales or any other business such as:
magazines, exams, radio interviews, theatre/TV work,
literary festivals, publishing house interest or other paid
work:

Esme Bates
8 East Street
Didcot
Oxford
OX11 8EJ
England
UK
M: 07710 474848
T: 01235 202517

Beside the lake,
Beneath the trees,
or on the loo.....
wherever you are reading this from,-
good for you!

Failing that, this anthology serves as a colouring-in book
or looks bright and jolly on your bookshelf.

Love yourself or how is anyone going to love you?
Dream.
Believe.
Achieve.

Esme Bates

Peace out,
E. J. Bates

Follow live broadcasts: on facebook

Good, Bad and Ugly Poems by E.J. Bates

Content

Good, Bad and ugly Poems by E.J. Bates

Hap-bee by E.J. Bates

In my favourite place in the world, my garden. Marvel
and find humour in the detail of nature. Beauty and
humour is all about you.

A bee! A bee!!
Is next to me!!!
Sipping lavender tea!!!!
This bee! This bee!!
Appears to be!!!!
very, very happpppp-bee!!!!!!!!!

Belgian Buns by E.J. Bates

Belgian Buns.
I love you so,
with your soft, comforting dough....
But your fats and carbs mean;
I should really say "No!"
But your tempting cherry beckons a tweek,
And your sugar icing makes me weak.
I try to walk by and not get stuck in-
But Belgian bun you are my biggest sin,
I get that urge, it is as though you scream,
"Take me now ..or there's that one with
cream!"
Taking a step outside the shop I gobble away,
Letting you have your deliciously wicked way!
Currants, cherry, cinnamon all are good,
Ooooooh.....I loves a belgian bun for my pud!

Happy Strong Year by E.J. Bates

A version of my poem was in the Oxford Mail, and liked by my oldest friend, Miki. A positive, motivational poem.

You are a tower of strength within and without,
You get knocked down, get up and keep standing,
You are a tower of strength within,
You don't drown in tears of pain and sorrow,
You let all burdens fall from your shoulders,
You hold your head high -others don't seem to care,
All anxieties slip from your mind,
You wake up smiling- regardless of the struggle,
Every shackle be loose you let,
You find a song to sing when there's no music,
Every shackle be loose,

You are a tower of strength within and without,
You give it all you've got when you have nothing left to give,
You are a tower of strength within,
You don't quit when everything within you is screaming at you "stop",

Good, Bad and Ugly Poems by E.J. Bates

You let all burdens fall from your shoulders,
You look at tomorrow with hope rather than fear and
doubt,
All anxieties slip from your mind,
You show your weakness in a perfect minded world,
Every shackle be loose you let you let.
Every shackle be loose.

You are a tower of strength within and without,
You are a tower of strength within,
You let all burdens fall from your shoulders,
All anxieties slip from your mind,
Every shackle be loose you let you let.
Every shackle be loose.

Berkshire Barks by E.J. Bates

Below is funnier if you read in a plummy voice. Historically recited on BBC Berkshire.

We all go to the toilet, this is true,
"Wee" in Berkshire is fed up of stepping in dog pooh!!
The Duchess should decree,
(on the topic of dog poo and wee)
"Remember that your dog's "meaty" poohs,
-are most definitely not desirable on one's shoes.
If he, in public, pooper,
Be sure to use your jolly, old scooper!"

The Green Man by E.J. Bates

Reading town centre got rid of a set of pedestrian lights on a very busy, major road. Councils seemed to be moving across to raised humps in the roads for pedestrians to

cross or zebra crossings. As a walking frame user, crossing the road at the time, I was interviewed on BBC South Today and BBC Berkshire. It was edited into a full monologue for radio, whereby the local MP had to go into the studio and justify their decision on this. One voice can promote change, always put your head above the parapet, if you see something that is not right. I wish I had performed this poem and to convinced

through humour; there is still no green light there.

Green Man don't die,
Help us- the passer-by
Your fatherly green glow,
Help us cross in rain, sleet or snow.

Green Man don't die,
Help us- the passerby,
Your fatherly digital clock,
Help us the blind, disabled -your flock.

Green Man don't die,
Help us- the passerby,

Your buses, taxis and vans must halt.
Help us with our no claims fault!

Green Man don't die,
Help us- the passerby,
we are a diverse and complicated fish,
we don't want post -mortems in a petri dish!

Du by E.J. Bates

I do my dose-

Blooooow!

Doff my duts up donce dore-

Coooough!!

I'm dull of dold do dee,

Dis dust dot dare.

Whiiiiimper!!!

Daching and demperature-

Doffing and deezing-

Dried demsiip and darmetocol,

Dothing dirks,

Dut dost of dall de droat deans I dannot deak,

My damily has had a deaceful deek!

Aaaaaaaaaaaaaaa-choooooo!!!!!

Good, Bad and Ugly Poems by E.J. Bates

13

Who is the Real Me? by E.J. Bates

This poem is designed to heal and centre, when we are at our lowest ebb. To encourage, motivate and heal. When your social and instinctive self are at odds and you need peace or to give yourself a good talking to.

Intelligent, adaptable and flexible,

The real me feels centred and held,

I feel earthed and grounded,

Our closeness and intimacy,

Evokes my trust and develops our connection,

My enjoyment and humour is increased in your presence,

I know who I am when I am with you,

We take each other seriously and make each other special,

You give me my sense of structure,

My social and instinctive self have stopped battling,

As with you I am always myself,

I am clean cut, protect and accept myself,

That is the real me

Ronnie by E.J. Bates

Inspired by a collection of photos on BBC Berkshire's site.

Mouth organ music you would play,

Brightening up every single day!

Motorbikes whizzing around bends,

Your ears you would always lend,

Who knew how this excitement would tragically end.

We decided it best you no longer drive,

We wanted you to be alive!

You were gracious in defeat,

Kept a motorbike photo you thought was "neat",

Then sharing a Kit Kat with me as a "treat",

Being the tea maker for us,

Maybe the odd trip on the bus.

Feeding you, to manage hunger and thirst,

The first hurdle our love would see,

Your mouth organ you forgot first-

Then lastly me.

Our biggest hurdle I would feel,

As I helped you drink and eat your meal.

You looked scared and confused one day,

The nurse came to reassure,

I touched your hand and would not go away,

Grieving inside how could I take more?

Five different shaped pills,

Was one of them making you ill?

As you were lit by the bedside light,

We adjusted your meds and decided to laugh and fight,

In my birthday card, you wrote the wrong name you did scribble and rewrite.

You may have forgotten you but I have not,

My darling man you are not forgot.

Evolution by E.J. Bates

All political parties made valiant points on the run up to the election. Meanwhile, on Utube Flynn conveys that he had found out that he had dementia 9 years ago; his garden was his sanctuary. Amongst all the battles between parties his colourful garden made me hope for the possibilities and opportunities of a coalition.

Farmer Flynn wore a blue tank top,

Refusing to accept his dementia "lot",

But grew beautiful things on his allotment plot,

Election time as we approach maverick May,

Please no violent revolutions over the next day,

(Evolution not revolution is Flynn's way.)

Make our garden a colourful array:

Red for tulips or roses,

Blue for pansy posies,

Yellow for daffs or maybe daisies,

Bit of green and other such colours,

Lots and lot of pretty flowers!

Free your heart from hatred.

Free your mind from worries.

Live simply.

Give more.

Expect less.

Left out by E.J. Bates

Broadcaster, Paul Ross, selected this poem to read out live on BBC Berkshire and cited it as his favourite poem in my collection.

Am I invisible?
Or just not here?
A hologram, a mirage,
Perhaps I have disappeared.

Maybe I am dreaming?
I don't think I smell.
Why is no one including me?
It feels like an empty hell.

Why can't they just accept me?
I want to play their games,
Instead they snigger and call me names.

I know I can't keep up with them,
I don't want them to shout or talk slow,
Just to let me feel they understand and know,
A chance to show I am just like them,
That I can be their fellow and their friend.

The Great Unwashed by E.J. Bates
Festival Memories...

one of my student's favourite poems. Also a chance for middle aged people to reminisce about being 16-18 years old.

Polka dot or fuchsia wellies,
Girls in shorts with lovely flat bellies,
But not washed for the weekend, so rather smelly!

Young men dressed in Marks and Sparks jeans,
But secretly- clothes- on their mums they still lean,
"Mum, this is the where the "in crowd" are seen!"

Lads prove their manhood this weekend by putting up.... a tent,
Building fires - we ponder on where our youth went:
Air guitars, heading banging and our hormone vent!

Police to musos ratio is high-
But dealers, touts and pickpockets pass by,

Good, Bad and Ugly Poems by E.J. Bates

"Hope they all stick together!" mother's sigh.

Every year it rains, which isn't funny,
Dear young souls pray for it to be sunny,
Revolting port-a-loos , that are no better than a
bushtucker dunny!

The usual coughs and colds Mum's fear,
"Why they don't change it so it's later in the year?
Gosh, I hope no one tries to sell them any gear!"

Expectations peak as they reach the gate,
Which band? Which stage? Where's my mate?
Quick! Red Hot Chili Peppers are on- let's not be late!

Young men stage dive,
Loving being alive,
Security checks: no gun, chain or knife!

Girl perched on rugby-playing shoulder,
The next generation brighter and bolder,
Carefully, she's gesturing and singing.....hold her!

Us: education, children, careers and wife,
Them: energy and enthusiasm- a zest for life,
No worries, creativity and humour: simply rife!

Out before them stretches poss-ib-il-ity,
Hopes and desires as epic as the sea,
What shared memories for you and me?

Grubby clothes soiled with smoke,

Some weirdo stranger offering you a line of coke?
You cannot believe it, surely a joke?
"No thanks mate I only drink the carbonated kind,"
He was clearly wasted, sozzled and out of his mind!
Let's Go! To your friend you sign!

In a wet tent you and a grubby hippy elope,
The pair of you have a cheeky grope,
All weekend, neither of you have used soap!

Monday draws to an end.
Leaving locals, slightly bitter,
To clean the mess and tidy litter,
We shut our sports facilities and gastro pub,
So we don't get germs and you don't eat all our grub!

Or truth we told are we just 'well jel',
That they are youths and we are in adult hell?
Their dreams, ambition and ideas,
Not cynical, hopeless and full of fears.
We call them the "great unwashed".
Or they just a younger version of us?

'Twas The....... by E.J. Bates

My partner's niece loves the original 'Twas The... poem. I wrote this for fun to amuse her. She especially likes the line about nanny's cheeky sherry! It is thought that youngsters are more stressed than our generation as they are glued to computers, instead of enjoying social activity.

'Twas the night before Christmas, and all through the home,
The devices at Natasha's were freezing and giving a moan,
The power was on and the screen bright,
In hopes that Natasha's presents would arrive that night.
She was logged on, her apps were loaded,
And clouds full to bursting, almost exploded;
While adding a Christmassy glow to the scene,

The lights on her iPad, flashed red, white and green.
when out on the drive there arose such a clatter,
Natasha ran to see what was the matter!
Away to the door she flew like a flash,
Forgetting her key in her christmassy dash.
She stood in the driveway and looked all about,
when the door slammed behind her, then locked out.
Then, on the drive what should appear,
But a Lapland -style sleigh and eight real reindeer,
And a little old man, who with scarcely a pause,
Chuckled: "My name is Santa..my last name is Claus."
Her iPad was startled, confused by the name,
Then it buzzed as it heard the old fellow exclaim:
"This is Dancer and Dasher and Prancer and Vixen,
And Cupid and Comet and Donner and Blitzen."
with all these odd names, it was puzzled anew;
It hummed and it clanked, and froze on view.
It searched on google, trying to "think";
Then the screen went on the blink.
unable to do its electronic job,
It said in a voice that was almost a sob:
"Your eyes - how they twinkle - your dimples so
merry,
Your cheeks so like roses, your nose like Nanny's
cheeky sherry,
Your smile - all these things, I've been programmed to
know,

But your name Santa and your address (devices can't lie),
Are things that I simply just cannot identify.
You've a jolly old face and a little round belly,
That shakes when you laugh like a bowlful of jelly;
My camera can see you, but still I insist,
Since you're not in my program, you cannot exist!"
Old Santa just chuckled a merry "ho, ho",
And sat down to type out a quick facebook or so.
The keyboard clack-clattered, it's tap sharp and clean,
As Santa fed this status into the machine;
"Put down your device!
It really is your evil vice!
Don't forget to list sporty toys-
That are healthy and good- for girls and boys,
Plus games to play on a dining room table,
That you can play with dear, old Auntie Mabel,"
Then he twittered on the machine saying "Merry Christmas" but with an emoji shrug,
Then had the sheer audacity to pull out the family's wi-fi plug!

Window Pane by E.J. Bates

.....when it's cold outside, when your world has fallen apart...especially for those who hate the winter and would hibernate, given the chance.

Season's wreckage through my frozen window pane,
Late Autumn fruit has long rotted now,
Gnarly ribs of trees are on view,
The sharp elbows and knees of their branches,
Dig in, aching, frozen against the bleak clouds,
Which bite red noses, chaff lips,
Runny eyes and raw hands.
The pain is too much.
I shut my curtain.
I think I'll stay in bed!

The Open Fire by E.J. Bates
To heal your soul, comfort your spirits and put 'fire in your belly'.

We light the match and light the paper,
The log catches light two minutes later,
The great throat of the chimney laughs,
Red logs beat with tropic heat,
Our tentacles uncoil,
We sit and stare at the dancing flames.
As the room fills with a dream blaze,
We are in a dream-daze,
The glow in our cheeks,
And relax for the first time in weeks.
Breath: calm, relaxed and meek.

Look Up and Around! by E.J. Bates

I would love to be commissioned to write adverts. I think this would be a fab advert.

As I look up from my screen, from this thing we call social,
I realise it is anything but authentic, caring or noble,
Twinkedin, Litter and other virtual, friend feeds,
But what are our real demands, commitments and needs?

When the door shuts -it's all an illusion,
Photos and posts are insane delusion,
Really they tell stories of isolation,
A robotic nation.
Everything appears shiny and glistening,
Is anyone really loving, caring or listening?

From since they were born,
Children think being robots is the norm,
Not skipping, climbing and playing on the lawn,
Does anyone still know the art of stringing   conkers
or   fishing   for

frog's born?

Can all Dad do is play with their child on an iphone or pad?
What happened to truth or dare and being a lad?
Don't stare at an inbox and flick on your phone,
Look up and out and ensure you have a home.

This way I promise you will never, ever feel alone.
To these children I say-
Children fall off your bikes!
Be a messy tyke!
Graze your knee and make a treehouse!
Do not just tip- tap away on that infernal mouse!

Closing the Blind by E.J. Bates

When I was at Oxford College I spent a summer offering art therapy at a Bosnian Refugee Camp in Slovenia. EVERY day somewhere in the world there is a war raging and thousands of refugees struggling. Unreported in the news and simply left to their own devices. It is as though we have drawn a blind down and chosen not to see this.

What blinds are drawn for the children of war?
Awkwardly rattling, junting, shuddering, shaking down,
Sightlessly feeling their way back to their deathbeds in the dark,
No rest, even at dusk, as nightmares pound pictures around their head,
Colourful fairy tale books turned to cinders,
Angry wolves mercilessly burn houses down—
As shining swords and bows hang from their parents' limp bodies.
No aristocratic princes on their imperial, white chargers to save the day.
No egg-shaped godmothers with tinsel wands.
Can any of us be the King's horses and men to put the war children back together again?
To close the blind on the children's living hell.

So Still by E.J. Bates
A poem to unwind with for mindfulness.

It's Friday and your working week ends.
Open a door, my dear, darling new friends.
I urge you to put your feet up and just sit down.
Relax, lower your blood pressure, let's get rid of that
weary frown.
So, still.

What can you hear if you open that door?
Bird song, trees rustling or a plane soar...
Maybe pipes are gurgling and there is an electricity
buzz?
So, still.

What can you feel where you sit?
Stroke the sofa's soft fibres, feel a calm setting in,
Feel the blood track your veins, and its' network within.
As your stressed mind settles, breath out a sigh,
wave away the week that has passed by.
So, still.

Give yourself permission to enjoy the peace-
That simple pleasure,
Allow yourself leisure,
Take a moment of peace, to interrupt life's flow,
To take a few minutes, to clear out your brain,
Before you jump up to resume normal service again.

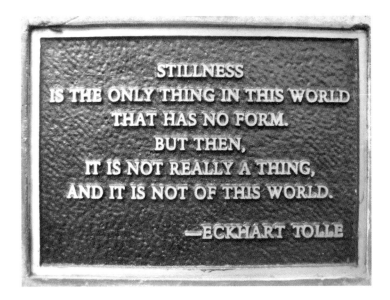

STILLNESS
IS THE ONLY THING IN THIS WORLD
THAT HAS NO FORM.
BUT THEN,
IT IS NOT REALLY A THING,
AND IT IS NOT OF THIS WORLD.

—ECKHART TOLLE

Things Are Never What They Appear by E.J. Bates
Do not always judge a book by it's cover.

Why do you look at me like that-
And label me simply as Fat?
Hard to find energy to exercise,
or resist easy food with tired eyes.
My tummy changed, it's gone all baggy,
My arms they flap, my boobs are saggy,
My muscles struggle as do my bones,
Fatigue and mobility makes me moan,
So how dare you think to point and sneer,
When you don't know what's gone on here,
Things are never what they appear.

Being an Oak Tree by E.J. Bates

Rooted feet, strong trunk and majestic branches. Go and hug a tree today!

"So you like drama?" Kyle quietly queries
"Do you pretend to be an oak tree?" he mocks,
"Swaying in the breeze!" he sarcastically scoffs,
"With your trees as branches!" he teasingly titters and retorts,

I don't react but smile,
(It must be difficult being Kyle.)
"Oh, being an oak tree,
Would be a wonderful thing to be!
You see:
If I was an oak tree I would grow stronger every year,
My feet with roots into the ground, that disappear,
I would sense the sun and push through in awe,
My legs the strong trunk pushing down into the floor,
I would grow taller, stronger and still keep going,
My arms the branches loose and flowing,
I would never stop,
My face the bird's nest where I would fly,

I would shoot for the sky!
I would bask and thrive in the sun,
Having so much fun!
Adding to my growth rings year after year,
Nothing that I would fear!
As my leaves unfurl-
In the sun I would be cosy, held and curl!

When the storm arrives and my leaves are wrenched
from me?
Leaving me bare and exposed?
My roots will run deep.
To stand strong against the winds pull,

When the other trees fall all around me,
With their shallow anchors,
There I would stand for another year,
oh, an oak tree,
Is a wonderful thing to be.

Foster Gran by E.J. Bates

Based of a life story of a teen I worked with. An interesting poem to maybe discuss notions of discretion and filters we use in social situations eg asking ourselves is this kind? Is this necessary to say?

To the Doctor my Mum cites:
"Jack's mouth carries on despite-,"
She says "He doesn't stop from dawn to dusk,
His words are ammunition to destruct and destroy,
Jack irritates and annoys-
He brings others into his lies,
He is "the devil "in my eyes.
He cheats , fights and steals,
Throws his food when he has a meal,"
She has gone up North and given the ADHD Doctor a long letter,
"Mum wants you to live with your Gran until you're better."

Good, Bad and Ugly Poems by E.J. Bates

Dyslexic Hero by E.J. Bates

Based on a conversation I had with a young person who reached out to me and told me he was self-harming. For sufferers and carers everywhere. This was published in a journal called Dyslexia Today. Everyone has a gift and strength. Nurturing the next generation of dyslexics to see their skills and talents is so important.

Sometimes it makes me so cross-
Dyslexia- makes me feel totally lost,
The Doctor gave me a lycra suit to wear under my uniform,
To stop me scratching my skin till I bleed when I am forlorn.
Now I try and pretend that I am a Dyslexic Superhero,
(Instead of a Dyslexic Looser, slash, Zero)

You see, at school I feel like I am falling down a large hole,
No fire exit. ladder or even a fireman's pole,
It's not like Alice in wonderland's rabbit hole,
With an English-speaking rabbit, playing cards and massive cats,
But cursing snakes, bad gambles and infectious rats,
Nor does it have a Queen of Hearts, flamingo sticks and jam tarts,
But queasy , circling black crows and stinky old –

In real life, my teachers tell me that "Dyslexics do quite well",
Examples of Inventors: Einstein, Curie and Bell,
Branson the Business tycoon and one of life's gents,
Picasso, warhol and others with a creative bent,
Google for yourself and you will see,
Dyslexic Heroes, determined-
but what about me?

Stinging by E.J. Bates
Mothers everywhere.

My mum was a local hero, when I was four,
Down a cycle path near where we lived, us sisters,
Mum sheared a bunch of nettles that covered the
floor,
As Nat had had cycled into them and was covered
in blisters!

Her wounded sobbing and tears echoed around the
neighbourhood.
Mum marched down the road, brandishing the shears,
Marched fearlessly to conquer the enemies that lay
in wait,
Mum furiously beheaded as many as she could,
There was no place for rest on mum's watch.
Just a funeral pyre of the fallen dead.

The next year the nettles raised their ugly heads
once more,
Their contorted heads spiky and threatening, covering
the floor,
The fierce parade lay in wait to attack again,
The evil enemy that would cause us pain,
we waited for Mum to charge once more,
To fight our battles and lay down the law ,
"They have grown again," she wearily complained,
But grabbed the shears, sighed and marched again.

Pickle by E.J. Bates
For my Mother

Not a chocolate or oyster.
I give you a pickle.
(You and Dad always call me one.)
Here.
Cheerful platinum loops wrapped in brown paper!
Promises heat.
Like the passion of your love.

It will catch your breath,
Like you my mother,
Its' fierce kisses will stay on your lips,
Possessive and strong like your arms,
It has layers that constantly surprise me,
And like you has a great big heart.

The Magic Cape by E.J. Bates

*For dear friends have health issues- keep hoping for
that cure and asking the right questions. NASA.*

The hero who had been to the moon three times.
The seventy year old jumped on stage with a hop and
a skip.
In his mind he was on top of the world looking down
upon us...

After his first journey he lost bone density and
muscle,
Unable to walk on his return,
But by his third visit NASA medicines and exercise
meant he recovered quickly.

With hopeful eyes I raised my hand and asked him
what lessons can we learn?
What does he know about MS?
He said he would look into it.
I have sent him this poem and live in hope.

Being Reborn by E.J. Bates

when you are miserable but then rediscover your 'mojo'.

What is this feeling?

Feeling as though I have been useful,

What is this feeling?

Feel as though I have helped people..

What is this feeling?

Feel as though I made some new, like- minded friends.

What is this feeling?

Feel as though I have had fun.

What is this feeling?

Feel appreciated by my boss.

What is this feeling?

It feels familiar- like an old friend.

Like good news.

Like relaxed.

Like excited.

Like being reborn.

Oh yes, I remember... happiness

I'm Not Sure What You Bring by E.J. Bates

For anyone who is being verbally abused by a boss
and feeling undervalued. For bosses who need to
learn to be leaders and trust people who are
different to them.

one, big step for man ..is to be kind-
To take people as you find,
will you find corruption, drugs, murder and mayhem
ensue?
or will you find out they are exactly like you?
Disabled, black or gay?
or middle-class, white and grey?
we all bring something to the table
Let's be kind, man, and enable.

Leaves on the Line by E.J. Bates
This happened to me just outside Reading Station!

Dozing off to snooze with hazy, happy thoughts,
Memories of the day purports-
My red bag upon my lap,
I have a little nap,

Cocooned in the cosy carriage,
Pub chats left behind of jobs and marriage,
Dream of fortune and fame,
Possibilities, opportunities and fair game,

I wake up, aware that something is near,
I open my eyes and peer,
I look down and my bag is not there,
Chilled, I look up and do not despair.
"Excuse me have you just stolen my bag, pet?"
(The man does not look like a threat.)

Good, Bad and Ugly Poems by E.J. Bates

He takes it out of his business laptop case.
(I should have reflected and used a mace!)
Instead the train pauses, it seems a lifetime,
I joke "What is the problem- leaves on the line!"
The train is delayed,
He paces; his temper is frayed.
He looks sweaty and stressed,
The train starts again and eases his distress,

We get off at Reading and he runs for the hills,
Too quick for any of the old Bill,
That pathetic man on the rob,
Strangely, my heart for him doth sob,
To the safety of fields and country zone,
To the promise and safety of my lovely home.

Age by E.J. Bates

As a baby, the discovery and milestones each day,
As a youth the expectation of the best days to come,
The excitement of the future,

And us, with our bitter, resentment of days gone by,
And disappointment of the past.

The grey-haired geriatric of the past,
The fossilised, infirm, useless, feeble....

But wait...

Maybe we are the white-haired, wise prophet,
The historic, well-lived soothsayer,

It is true...

The spirited skip of the future,
The new, fresh, enthused.

But often...

The clumsy, confused, pupil,
The uneducated, rude and naive child.

Yes, the thrill of a new chapter,
But there is comfort of a book already read..

Yes, the freshness of a new, green space,
But there is interest of the historical, classic, ancient ruin...

The wispy, engagingly eccentric is age,
The stylish, wise and strong.
One can cringe at the inexperienced work,
The storytelling IS better by the old or infirm.
The green young shoots not yet developed,
But the established plants hold their colour and shape,

It is true, there is dread of death and decay in the future,
But birth can be enjoyed and celebrated by us.

Booze Bus Battle by E.J. Bates

For a dear friend who tragically lost her son due to the lack of education among young people as regards drink driving. Such a tragedy to a beautiful family.

Trafalgar. Waterloo. Reading on a Friday night.
Slashed. Plastered. Hammered. Slaughtered.
Faced. Wasted. Tipsy. Sozzled. Wrecked.
"Toot! Toot!" parps the Booze Battle Bus as it swings into a layby.
Paramedics helps wounded soldiers on the bar battlefield,
Absorbing heavy drinkers on a Friday and Saturday night,
Pastors patrol the streets like Red Cross volunteers,
Scooping up victims of booze and depositing them to the makeshift ward.

Depression. Liver Damage. Brain Damage. STDs.
Teenage Pregnancy. Violent Attacks. Aggressive Behaviour,

General crime and disorder.
Toileting and vomiting over our Ladies of the Lamp.

23,350 people were seriously injured last year from drink driving,
590 people were killed in drink-drive related incidence,
Alarmingly the peak age was 18.
Underaged drinking is also on the rise 29% of 12-17 year olds involved in any sort of anti-social behaviour had been drinking,
16% of school children who have committed crimes have done so under the influence of alcohol,
Nearly 1/3 of pregnant 15-18 year olds had been drinking before sex,
Sadly 40% of 13-14 year olds were drunk when they first had sex and regret it,
13% of 16-18 year olds used contraception while drunk compared to 75% while sober.

How can we keep our loved ones safe?
1. Do not EVER drink and drive.
2. Make sure you eat before drinking.
3. Don't mix different alcoholic drinks.
4. Don't mix alcohol and drugs/medicine. (check with Doctor if you can drink with your meds)
5. Don't leave your drinks unattended.
6. Only use licensed taxis.
7. Keep hydrated by drinking water/soft drinks.
8. Keep track of the amounts of units.
9. Don't walk home alone.
10. Stop when you have had enough.

If someone collapses step forward for First Aid:
1. Get someone to dial 999
2. Put them in the recovery position
3. Check breathing'.
4. Keep them warm.
5. Stay with them.
6. Wait for an ambulance

Some other shocking statistics to make us think twice:
1,000 annual suicides a year are attributed to alcohol.

Potty IQ by E.J. Bates

A near death experience at an American Park reminded me of the meaning of life. Queuing seems to be a western past-time.

First IQ down the road,
Then IQ for the car park Q,
After that I Q in the carpark for a car space,
Then I IQ in the car park for a car park ticket,
Phase one of Qing complete.
We are here.

Phase Two.
Next IQ for the ticket to the whole amusement park,
Then IQ for the entrance ticket to Q ,to the particular area of the park I need to go to,

Next stage of Qing I am told I need to Q at a computer,
It is really silly now,
Basically I am Qing for a touchscreen to enable me to
Q for a ride, with in an area, within park !!
Q within a Q, within a Q, within a Q ,within a , Q, within a Q, within a , within a Q within-
wait!
Q for the Harry Potter Q.
AUTHORISED.
Phase Two of Qing over.

Phase Three.
On the homeward straight now....
Qing empty faces,
we Q against a backdrop of gargoyles, turrets, black silhouettes,
A 2 hour Q.... the sign says!!!!
My god, I have already Q'd for 2 hours!
Weary in my ECV having clocked 2 miles by now,
I corner the Harry Potter look-alike- Tour Guide,
A pale faced, world weary chap,
He wants us to jump the Q!
Bless his heart, or so I thought.
He heads us through some sort of Potter labyrinth.
I am uneasy.
I know nothing else now bar Qing.

So we are on the ride now.
A roller coaster in the dark.
Riding on a broomstick,

Diving,
Spinning,
Whirling,
Giddy,

Phase Four.
Can you guess the next Q?
You've got it
Q First Aid
Q Paramedic
Q A and E
Qing to be dizzy, sick, unable to speak, paralysed
Qing for heaven.

Phase Five
I have flashback of all the Qs in my life-
Jobs.
Qing for a better one.
Family.
Qing for kinder.
Relationship.
Qing for perfection.
My god, is life one big Q??
We are forever Qing.

Potty IQ.
Moral of the story: Be careful of what you Q for and
enjoy every single day in the here and now.

Fear of Flying by E.J. Bates

written for an acquaintance who was dreading a flight.

Take off gets faster and faster,
wink, nudge enjoy that plane being your master,
Comfy clothes and a bottle of water,
Be your own Mother and not like a daughter,
Snuggle down and watch your favourite movie,
Forget everything else and be lovely!

If you still feel bad put on your light,
Plane phobia is your fight,
If it is bumpy ask them if they can find out when it
will pass,
Explain you feel stressed and can cope if they tell
you how long it will last.

Life changes: health, birth, death, marriage, divorce, or
graduation,

Promote fears and phobias of flying from our great nation,
They say expose yourself to computer simulation,
How a plane flies......
in the great skies?
Medicines can reduce anticipatory anxiety,
But it is suggested chatting and reaching out to our society.

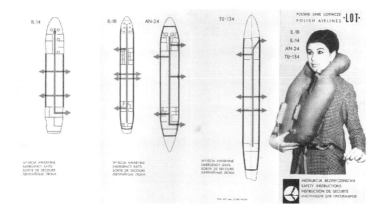

Webs by E.J. Bates

For a dear family friend who had a lifelong fear of spiders, as do her entire family!

Do you have a virtual spider on your screen?
It may help you to stop you thinking that they are mean.

You scream, cry, have trouble breathing, sweat and your heart–

Is it something from our ancestors that we feared to survive?
Be reassured that Chile, Colombia, Costa Rica and others eat spiders to keep alive!

"Imagine situations involving spiders" they say,
"Watch others hold spiders as they play,"
Get a virtual spider, as I have said,
And put that phobia to bed?

Deal by E.J. Bates

The trials of the start of a new relationship.

After having a pooh-pooh,
ALL I am simply, politely requesting is...scrub the loo.

What do you mean it is a job for you?!

Right, whilst we are on the subject of health-
Please just tidy up after yourself.
There is not a cleaning, magical elf,
The dishwasher does not load itself,
Stuff does not automatically fly onto a shelf.

.......what do you mean I am beautiful and thin?

No, no, no....whilst we are on the subject of sin:
Full hands out of a room and full hands in,
Please Honey, just do something... like put out the bin,
Your clothes are growing legs,
Please Honey, just brush your toothy pegs,
Also wash out your cup of shmegs and dreggs-

........why are you winking and saying you always make the beds?
No, I am not "a nag bending your earlobe",
Not asking you to re-invent the globe!
Merely wanting to not tidy up all day,
Just wanting some things MY way!

You are sorry, you say?

I love you too, I just wish-
Maybe I am selfish,
Maybe I am fishwife,
But I really want us both to enjoy our life!
Not live in squalor and strife!

You are asking me out for a meal?
You are sorry for how I feel?

My love, yes BUT do we have a deal?
Before my heart, you doth steal!

The Big Issue Seller by E. J. Bates
Inspired by a friend.

I spent a bit of time chatting to Kevin Mac,
Fallen on hard times - trying to get back on track,
He had kicked his habit, to get his life back,
He had learnt of a life outside of booze and smack!

A funny, honest and upbeat clown,
But I saw people walked past him with their heads'
down-

Why did you do that?
Why not stop and have a chat?

Did you offer £2.50 for his magazine?
Or is your budget a bit too lean?
Or even say an acknowledging Hi?
Or maybe simply make contact with your eye?
Or just say thanks but no thank-you and bye?
Or were you just another passerby?

Not feeling sorry for himself , or giving up, is his way,

He stands there hoping to make everyone's day,
By giving them a smile regardless of whether or not
they pay,

He doesn't consider himself as char-it-y,
In 45 minutes he made a poultry two pounds fift-y!
Pays for his Big Issues himself and makes one pound
twenty-five,
For each one he sells, that money, keeps him alive.

I gasped and pitied -much to Kevin's mirth,
He laughed saying, "He was not dead and this was his
re-birth,
Everyone has something to be miserable about,"
"Big Issue" he did happily shout, shout, shout!
"Realise when you have done wrong.
Change the record to your new song!"

Gargoyle by E.J. Bates
The ugliness of being betrayed.

I see several bodies with one head,
I see a body with several heads.
Why are grotesque, stone monsters' eyes hanging on
cloisters staring down on the influencers as they
study?
Why are they so eerie, ghoulish and bloody?
What is the meaning of these diseased winged,
monkeys, these strange savage lions, and nightmarish
lambs?
To what purpose are these creatures, half beast, half
gentleman?
What do they tell us about man's natural state?
Do they warn of power, greed and man's possible
fate?

Both him and his lover - family men.
A man so witty, kind, clever and true,
How could he do this? Do this to you?
Two heads and one body or one body with two
heads.
Whichever which way he took a man to bed.
Was it the drink? Was it the drugs?
Such a smashing gent acting like a thug.
I wish you luck, I really do,
Do what is best,
Best for you.

HMS by E. J. Bates
Trying to keep afloat.

Jane did not like being away from home,
Staying in a hotel, gosh, she did moan....
She may as well been out at sea,
She was miserable and as homesick as can be.

A vodka martini and a sleeping pill,
Made her feel more at home and less ill.
Trying to sleep in an over- warm room after a meal.
After food that ran around in her tummy like an
electric eel.

She slept between the sheet and duvet,
Hoping her heat-induced anxiety would go away.

Pretending she was an adventurer out at sea,
But still as lost as can be.

Smorgasbord of buttery stains nudged against her
skin,
She requested new towels and insisted on decent
bed linen.
Housekeeping staff discussed the X Factor at 7am!
on HMS Victory she would have found less seamen!

Punctuated by a lift closing and opening,
Sleep was a rare and beautiful thing,
She tried to imagine the squeak was a seagull sing!
Little did she know what the journey was the following
year,
She got her tests back and it was everything this sea
dog feareed

A year of chemo and an intensive cancer drug,
Cabin fever and si8ck as a sea dog
She dragged herself through the year like boat tug
She stated recovery with a gentle jog,
But collapsed in a heap with an almighty sob

The journey was hard with lots of icebergs at sea,
But now she is sea -faring again, on a cruise, with
her family and me.

At the End of the Day by E.J. Bates

Your teens and twenties days are rather crap,
worrying about: who said this, who said that,
As you get older it is plain to see
what will be
will simply be,
At the very end of the day-

we all end up the same way!

DIY by E. J. Bates
Home renovation.

We are rubbish at Do It Yourself innovation,
So employed men- ones good at renovation,
Googling tradesmen, to the computer we went,
Keeping an eye out for ones with an artistic bent.

Things I learnt over the year,
Keep alert with nose, eye and ear,
This warning I give to you,
(As someone who went for a month without a working
loo)

If builders plaster your ceiling and wall,
Heating needs to be off so it doesn't crack at all,
Or it needs to be redone,
(It is so muddy and not much fun.)
Don't do-it-yourself but get a proper painter

Do not be a fool,
(You are no Andy Warhol.)

Check sparky has a certificate and earths your mains,
or touching switches and sockets will cause you pains.

Check builder wears a helmet in case they fall.
Whilst they are knocking down a retaining wall,
watching a man disappear under through the floor,
Means he will be off work- as he is rather sore.

I could go on but you get the idea,
You really have nothing to fear!
But they frequently leave early or are late,
whilst insist on calling you their friggin' "mate".
They will stop you making DIY disasters that's for
sure,
You will get addicted and want to renovate more and
more!

As for living without a loo for five week,
That is another poem on which I will speak!

Stomach Fat by E.J. Bates

Some pacey words to encourage my steps towards weightloss.

HEAL your joint,
Stay on point.
SLOW ageing of skin,
Bonus will be thin.
Diabetes prevent,
Give body air and vent.
Normalise blood pres-sure,
weigh and mea-sure.
Protect brain health,
Nature's wealth.
Supercharge energy,
Be the best you can be.
Fix Your digestion,
Cancers and all sorts a crap I forgot to mention.
BOOST -
Your Sluggish-
Metabolism.

Sugar and Fat by E.J. Bates

You give me energy for a little bit,
Then one minute later I feel like death,
You make me surge, excited and feel alive,
Until my sugar levels take a near fatal, catastrophic dive,
I then feel sick, am angry, detest myself and full of hate,
You are two-faced-
And not my mate,
You surge through my blood with an unstoppable force,
I am sad and depressed when you have run your course,
You leave me bloated and drag me down to my lowest ebb,
Looking and feeling like a greedy pleb, sugar and fat,
You pratt,
You make me high,
But it really, really is time that I say good-bye!

Good, Bad and Ugly Poems by E.J. Bates

Coffee by E.J. Bates

In a crisis "streaking off to make some tea!"

Used to the English war-torn, vicar's wife way "to be",

But what with cappuccinos and lattes,

Cost-a-lot or Star.... bucks is now the modern way.

Neigh cup and saucer or even an urn,

The common tea we thus spurn,

Instead a cup and lid en plastique,

Addictive two shots- never milky and weak.

But the things that fascinates me most about the common coffee shop-

Is that whilst other retail units close and flop,

More and more coffee shops are rising to the top,

Maybe selling a moment in time to sit, ponder and stop.

Reading Bridge is Falling Down by E.J. Bates

Stuck in a traffic jam

Reading Bridge is falling down,

Falling down, falling down,

Reading Bridge is falling down,

Reading Borough Council.

Build a bridge with steel 'n' that,

Steel 'n' that, steel 'n' that,

Build it up with steel 'n' that,

Reading Borough Council.

One bridge is not enough,

Not enough, not enough,

One bridge is not enough,

Reading Borough Council.

Sick of Qing in my car,

in my car, in my car,

Sick of Qing in my car,

Reading Borough Council

I am now late for work,

late for work, late for work,

I am now late for work,

Reading Borough Council

Build a second bridge while you're at it,

while you are at it, while you're at it,

Build a second bridge while you're at it,

Reading Borough Council.

Tomorrow I will walk or cycle,

walk or cycle, walk or cycle,

Tomorrow I will walk or cycle,

Reading Borough Council

Do you want us to use your buses?

use your buses, use your buses,

Do you want us to use your buses?

Reading Borough Council.

Will I have to stand up on the bus?,

on the bus, on the bus,

Will I have to stand up on the bus?

Reading Borough Council.

Can men work through the night?

through the night, through the night

Can men work through the night?

Reading Borough Council.

Suppose the men should fall asleep?

fall asleep, fall asleep,

Suppose the man should fall asleep?

Reading Borough Council

Give the men tea and chocolate biscuits,

Tea and chocolate biscuits, tea and chocolate biscuits,

Give the men tea and chocolate biscuits,

Reading Borough Council.

Concrete Love by E.J. Bates

The med glistened azure blue,

we looked out wistfully out far,

Just me and you,

we had taken the chair out in the car,

How were you feeling blue, off par?

"You know water droplets", you finally speak,

"I feel really sorry for the droplets banging against concrete,"

You said it happily almost profoundly,

So glad you are on my side and my family.

Haven't They Recounted Yet? By E.J. Bates

written the night of the election.

Haven't they recounted yet?

The conservatives are in, I bet,,

It's all over the TV,

Had a chuckle to myself, he, he,

Drifted in and out of sleep last night,

Listening to the theatre of election night,

SNP have basically staged a takeover of Scottish isle,

Nicola not happy that Cameron is the leading man, by any mile,

Twenty year old politician thanks his mummy and daddy,

Boots out an established politician, Alexander, 'the baddy',

Loads of labour politicians have lost their jobs,

Cameron is Prime Minister, is this our best of a bad mob?

Big Boned by E.J. Bates

Father Christmas, a 'bigger boned' man,

(As he had gone totally off plan,)

Chocolate roulade with extra cream,

Pigs in blankets, with bacon, that was *not* lean,

All swilled down with a Sherry or two,

The poor chap was full of constipated...**pooh**

Off to 7pm Slimming world he did **go**,

With a skip and a merry.. ho,ho.

He knows he has probably put on this week,

As he has some lifestyle changes he has to tweek,

He filled up his freezer of slimming world meals,

He swotted up on free and speed food that fills,

Good, Bad and Ugly Poems by E.J. Bates

He exercised a bit more each day,

He slowly found his issues melt away,

Instead of feeling ill and fat the following **year**,

He embraced the season with love and a.. cheer!

Special Thanks by E.J. Bates

To my Mark,
with much love,
To bosses who boldly believed,
To critics who were cuttingly cruel.,
To students who sublimely succeeded,
To mentors who motherly mended,
To friends who were flippin' fun,
To family who fondly fed me,
(Trying saying that after a glass or two!)
You are all special in so many ways,
Recalling our friendship,, fun and carefree days!

Would you like to receive information about the work of E.J.Bates? Or maybe you are a book seller or agent keen to get involved?

We need you!

Mailing List

Name:

Address:

Email:

Tel. No.

To: Esme Bates, 8 East Street, Didcot, OX11 8EJ, UK

Printed in Poland
by Amazon Fulfillment
Poland Sp. z o.o., Wrocław